MIRACLE
IN
SPACE

MIRACLE IN SPACE

STANLEY TOWNSEND

CITIOFBOOKS, INC.
3736 Eubank NE Suite A1
Albuquerque, NM 87111-3579
www.citiofbooks.com
Hotline: 1 (877) 389-2759
Fax: 1 (505) 930-7244

Ordering Information:

Quantity sales. Special discounts are available on quantity purchases by corporations, associations, and others. For details, contact the publisher at the address above.

Printed in the United States of America.

ISBN-13:   Softcover   979-8-89391-959-2
        eBook   979-8-89391-960-8

Library of Congress Control Number: 2025920570

TABLE OF CONTENTS

PROLOGUE

It was in the month of December very close to Christmas when this happens. For there was a first time in space history was made when two space launches happen at the same time. This would be the only time it was a secret kept away from the world because interest in space exploration was almost gone due to disaster that took so many lives. Then the world voted universally to stop exploring space.

This was the government answer to ensure the safety of everyone. That was four years ago and now two companies wanted to go so much back out into outer space. One company made a space station while the second worked on a bold and daring plan. Which was kept in private and not to be known due to wishes of this unknown donor.

Then there was a young man named Sheldon who was a space engineer whom loved history and space got the backing of this and very wealthy and unknown donor who alone gave the green light. To build on this second plan and have it ready on a minutes notice.

Now our story begins with many twists in telling this tale.

CHAPTER I

THE NEW SPACE STATION DEVON SEVEN

There were advances made in space exploration that allowed the very young to be in beyond earth. Now there was a brand new space station built by a private space company to place kids in outer space. It looked like the old Skylab Space Station from a long time ago now with advances built in. About this new station held only twelve people and its sole purpose was teaching kids about science. Also to be a pioneer for kids in helping to learn all about outer space. This time there was only eleven people on board. There was a beautiful woman placed in charge of the station back on earth, and her name is Andrea McBride, This woman had her own dreams of being in outer space one day and yet, She has a deep secret that no one knows about.

This one lady was fair and gave no favor to any kids that was on board. The children aboard had the shortest time in space before they had to come back down to earth. This was one of the conditions that the private space company had in place. For it was their very own golden rule and the only law in space and on earth. Andrea's husband named D. Maynard McBride was very moody man for being in outer space and had very deep regrets. Toward his marriage to this one woman, yet he had a deep secret as well. In time his intentions will be known and very severe and hard to understand"Why"

Back down on Earth at Cape Canaveral, There was two rockets on the launch pad getting ready for a future space launch. At first there were tech. problems that had to be worked out in time. Now this new company had the blessings from the President. For on the first and second rocket there was a top secret cargo that alone the highest priority of all.

About this new space companies Bee Space and Dark Star they worked together on the joint venture. Dark Star built the space station while Bee Space made something new in a worst place deal hoping never to use it. A Space Rescue, ever since that awful day long ago. No one ever had the urge to build and explore space until now.

Bee Space was named for a pioneer in Space Exploration. Astronaut Bee Moon who founded this new company and used her mega inheritance of ninety billion dollars from her late uncle. To build it and caught the attention of a young space engineer named Sheldon who is now working for now.

Dark Star space company built the space station in honor of promoting science. Ever since the past advances in space exploration came to be. It was Bee Moon own idea to promote science in outer space. To promote women in space and it was her own bold move that caught Andrea McBride. To become the first teacher in outer space in time; But she had a one term before going up, That her husband D. Maynard McBride would be coming also and he was also a space pilot himself. This one move that the couple made would place a divide in their relationship. Aboard the space station Devon One that has only one shuttle craft ready to leave at a minute notice.

Back at Cape Canaveral NASA commander Abner S. Peabody a man in charge of all missions going out to space. Learns of something very important to him. That causes him to think very hard in a fight of good vs evil. That was on his desk a mega life insurance policy so close to ten trillion dollars if the Space station was destroyed by an act of GOD. In this fight evil will win at this time and he begins to think on a plan. To make it happened but, Abner needed help like many partner's to go along with him.

So he got started talking to a D. Maynard McBride about a his very evil plan. In time this man would be tempted to leave the space station. Even when it meant to leave Andrea all alone with the kid. In the grand and final act of betrayal in the matters of greed not love anymore.

CHAPTER II

SHELDON AND GEORGE

These young and great men were to be destined to place their own mark in history. Sheldon Muddle and his older brother named George begin their work. For Bee Moon Space agency on a new idea which got the backing of their Uncle Myron J. Muddle who wanted so much to be anonymous. For their was two space rockets that had super secret cargo inside. That got the President of the United States himself to look in. To this very secret cargo and about this one man. He was heard but never seen up close. But there was only two people at NASA whom seen him in person. That was Bee Moon and Myron J. Muddle himself and all they would ever say to the public when asked. "He is a very busy Man"

The brothers one time got into a fight and Bee Moon step in to stop it. She alone told the brothers"Get along and worked together or be FIRED right on the spot."! Since I am paying you two triple wages, I have this right to tell you. Sheldon Muddle was in shocked when he heard this from Mrs. Bee and George Muddle took this lady very serious. Because she talked to"Great Chief"and got some mean plans for revenge. You know that"Aunt Bee is a native woman.

Now George and Sheldon Muddle begin working on the space rockets together. George was given the highest honor in working on Rocket One, Sheldon worked on the Rocket two. The brothers learned one thing so very true,"Do not make Aunt Bee mad she is serious and mean". They both agreed to called Mrs. Bee that in order to show great respect to her.

Then there was a meeting that everyone attended and it dealt with keeping secrets. From family and and especially friends. Mrs. Bee Moon had a message for all and it crossed many lines so personal freedoms to some. Whom alone take it the wrong way and wanted so much to walked out. But being paid triple wages made all the critics listen. What the boss had to say"Ladies and Gentleman This Space Mission is very top secret. Like a D-Day secret way back in Word War 2 type of deal. That is how big your job is here at Cape C.

Sheldon Muddle ---------   --"Whoa that is big and how did she know I have a problem keeping a secret."!

George Muddle --------------"Dang this is big"

Then Bee came to both Sheldon and George and told them to put this on their ankles. That was a new ankle monitor only good at the Cape C. For it had a microphone attached to the monitor and if they ever told a secret out in the open. They both would get the living daylights shocked out of them. George Muddle knew to keep secrets, but Sheldon had problems. This young man had a terrible time keeping a secret. Which made Bee come forward and open in a safe room to talk.

Gentleman You two are involved in a very top secret mission like a D-Day deal. But all I can say is to eased your mind."A Outer Space Rescue"

That is why you two are placed here at the Cape Canaveral for the next two months and then after take a very long vacation. You can go anywhere and do what's ever your heart wants. Then the brothers talked to Bee

Sheldon ------------------"Comic Con I am going to miss this event."

George -------------------"Hunting and Fishing"

Then Bee spoked to Sheldon and then to George

Sheldon ----------------- Comic -Con is once a year deal and there will be other Comic book conventions.

You will have all access pass to comic book places and movie studios. But right now I need you here !

George ----------------- You will get a all expense paid three months of fishing and hunting in Alaska.

But if you waste a hunt or fishing by killing a monster white tail deer and leave it. then you will lose the rights and have to leave fast.

The rights of hunting and fishing on a island that is near five hundred acres.

It is my own island that I inherited.

George -------------------- No Aunt Bee this is very good news for me and I wont waste it.

Bee -------------------- George"You can call me Aunt Bee at anytime"When my younger sister named Mary Ann married a super rich man and got the money. They both spent time in outer space and when that dang thing blown up and I lost her. I was robbed of the chance to become a Aunt. Then when you call me

"Aunt Bee"that made my day here. You will be working on the first rocket and Sheldon you will be on the second. Sheldon threw a fit and wanted to be number one. But Bee put him in his place fast and gave this young man a super rare comic book panel. It was from the hottest comic at that time.

Sheldon accepted to be number two because Bee got thru to him fast. Both men worked together and never threw any more fits of rage. Since their new boss was amazing wealthy and the dreams of a private hunting / fishing for George. Then for Sheldon a pass to the comic book places and movie studios made his day as well. There was on more thing that Mrs. Moon made very clear to Sheldon and this man had to listen."NO CELL PHONES or CAMERAS ARE ALLOWED"!

At the comic book places or movie studios especially and this was to be enforced by a big man named"Howard"whom Sheldon alone respected very deeply.

When George Muddle got in touch with Dad, He told him just one thing.

Me and Sheldon are now working at the Cape Canaveral and when my vacation comes up. I want to take you for a hunting and fishing trip in Alaska,"Please bring Mom along as well".

Mrs. Muddle passes out when she alone hears this good news from George.

Sheldon Muddle did not have a girlfriend at this time. Yet in the background at Cape Canaveral, There was a very beautiful lady working at the space agency now. Looking at him with the words she said in silence, I'll am watching you Sheldon.

Both men worked on the rockets and getting them ready for a future launch into space.

George was looking forward to the endless hunting and fishing adventure. He told this one thing toward a future father in law about hunting and fishing in Alaska. That won the great man over to his side. For George was in love with a beautiful woman her name was"Mercy".

Sheldon attended a comic book convention and caught the attention of a beautiful lady wearing a Spider Gwen suit and she came to him and slapped her hand on his behind. This one act caught Sheldon by surprise and he went back to the Cape Canaveral and all alone worked harder on his rocket. Because he was inspired by greater things, George well he was only thinking about the hunting and fishing trip with a lady named"H. Mercy Meins"and her parents.

Sheldon was ahead of George on his rocket and started to brag to his older brother. Then he got his smart phone and got caught by his brother. It would be the only time that George Muddle was very bitter and MAD. At Sheldon and took his smart phone and smashed it into a thousand pieces with a little help from liquid nitrogen poured on it.

George told his little brother just three things,"You big dummy I am not losing my Alaska trip and my date with"H. Mercy Mains".

I will get you a brand new smart phone and pay for one year of service FREE.

"Now lets get back to work on this"!

Sheldon gave up his smart phone and stayed busy working and helped George along the way.

CHAPTER III

MRS. ANDREA MARIE JONES MCBRIDE

From four years ago to now in the month of November so very close to"Thanksgiving". This is story of beautiful young woman who was the only daughter of a Politian. His named was Max Jones whom was always in the spotlight, But Andrea was growing up in the public eye. She alone hated so much to be in the spotlight, which drove her away from her only father. Then on such fight became the final straw in their relationship. When she asked her father to get a smartphone and he balked and said"NO WAY and NEVER TO HAPPEN "

Because this one man loved a flip phone so much that he invested. In the cell phone company that had service to one. For this man it was the only way he can have a very private talking on the phone deal. Mr. Jones studied American history so much and remembered the lessons of the past. Then he worked his way in the spotlight when became the governor. To the state of Nevada and this time without his daughter by his side.

For she has chosen to be with her husband D. Maynard McBride. This were to be a sore spot for a time and, Mr. Jones asked the news media to leave her alone. They did just that and for Andrea there was going to be peace in her life now."No more ever being in the spotlight to everyone."Now in the present time there was a opportunity to go into outer space and D. Maynard McBride signed Andrea up and the kids up as well without talking to her first. Her own life was going to be changing so very fast. Because

There were advances in space exploration that made it possible for children. Young as five years old to be in outer space and this was not or never welcomed. In Andrea's world cause her loving husband a space pilot himself and an idiot on rare times. Then it happen D. Maynard just taken his only kid up in space a girl and didn't tell Andrea about it."WOW"she was very mad at him and called out his full name.

"Dick Maynard McBride"you idiot, This came at a time when she was trying to give up swearing. Especially in public and it began was the seed of distrust between him and life all around. Now she had to go into outer space herself and get her little girl back down on earth.

NOW ALL ABOARD THE SPACE STATION DEVON SIX I

D. Maynard McBride was there with his one child and he brought up three more. In less than two weeks this man just broke Moon space agency protocol. He was on the verge of getting fired and black ball from being a space pilot. For Bee Moon founder and enforcer of rules in her own company. This one idiot of a man was heading for the final act of deep horror where there was no such return or forgiveness of any kind.

BACK AT CAPE CANAVERAL II

D. Maynard McBride just got another ride heading back to outer space. This time would not be so good for the truth. To be told when Andrea woke up just in the space station,and just seen her daughter aboard and this place and this one lady was"SO MAD at her husband for bringing up a five year old into space. To her deep surprise there were three more kids aboard, Twin Native American children that were 8 and what set them apart from any was, They were different and yet very special. Then the last child was a young British Girl named"Mary"she was ten years old. Life aboard the space station was very simple the older kids was taught science and did experiments and worked to make life better for the younger kids. Andrea was still very MAD at her husband for doing this very wrong act of all. Very deep down in her own heart she had a very bad feeling come over. That she needed to stock up on supplies and find a way to get off this station for good.

AT CAPE CANAVERAL III

Aunt Bee called George into her office and told him to take off for three days. Then after his time was up, He had to report and see"GREAT CHIEF"as soon possible. For a possible trip into Outer Space and had to ready in a minute notice. This made George's day and Sheldon overheard the news and he was so MAD.

Then Aunt Bee just called"Howard"in and there was no more fits from this young man. Then Aunt Bee then called Sheldon in and told him that he will needed on ground control.

He will be helping out everyone there at the right time, but if he messed up then"Howard will have a good day"

Sheldon --------------"gulp as he swallowed down his smoothie"

George Muddle invited his love"H. Mercy Meins"to visit him in a public place. To have a well meaning full talk as friends. She loved the idea because it was a sign of change. That was very honorable from him and there was no more talk behind close doors. George started this talk about naming the rocket he was working on.

"Angelina"But he had to settle on Angel One to keep peace with H. Mercy Meins She was so very MAD at him for thinking about another woman just to have him. Yet George came back and said with a strong voice in his words.

"Angelina is my best friend in the army and she fell in battle. I wanted to honor her memory by naming this rocket so in spirit be with the stars.

Mercy overwhelm by this noble deed she hugged very hard George dearly and wouldn't let go. Then she said to him"I Love You "

Their own love will be stronger from this moment on. In time change will be coming for both of them.

CHAPTER IV

COMING TOGETHER

When Mercy pledge her own love to George for doing something beautiful. This was because her family was in the military and their own roots run deep in the marine corp. She was Simper Fi all the way and respected George on what he was doing. On the other side of Cape Canaveral. Sheldon Muddle learns of the identity of a woman who alone had a crush on him.

This beautiful woman wanted so much to get Sheldon, to notice her. So she took a self picture of herself in the Spider Gwen outfit on.

Then wrote a note saying, Tonight I want to meet you in person "A Friend"She got the idea from watching for the first time."Superman the movie 1978"

SHELDON MUDDLE MEETS HIS FRIEND I

It was on a Saturday when this young man receives a handwritten note in cursive writing. It was from a lady and it had a photo of

Spider Gwen along with it. This made Sheldon very nervous and scarred at the same time. But the scientist side of him realized that it was his only chance to find peace, So he went along with it. So he read the note alone and the time of the meeting was to be at seven pm.

While he was working on his rocket a beautiful lady came in and said. "Hello Dr. Sheldon my name is Elana and I was Spider-Gwen in the past. The news made him stopped working and took sudden notice of this very beautiful woman. Then Elana started to talk and this one man wanted to listen with open ears and mind. For Elana she was a woman of science also and loved Marvel comics and Disney. But her first love was science and Moon space agency wanted her for that. Yet the comics was to be her second love and hoping to get Dr. Sheldon Muddle. In the grounds of dating and future romance with this one man, That made her one heart give in to loved this very impossible man. Yet it was"Howard the man"Sheldon assistant made this love match to be. Flash back right into

GEORGE MUDDLE AND MERCY MEINES II

The young woman named"Mercy"Her full name is H. Mercy Meins and when she came into this world. She was a very beautiful baby girl whom turn out to be very beautiful young woman. While she was growing up in school the boys called her"Have Mercy"this was a mean thing to say. But Mercy never gave it any thought about it. Then at the later years of school she took up self defense classes and men respected her very much. But it was George Muddle whom alone showed her and very deep and meaning love that was very rare.

All this man ever seen was the inside of her and that is what made this woman's day. Because he alone loved the inside of a lady that is the heart and soul now. It was because a battlefield injury on George that was very deep and very personal to him. Yet, It was his commander Lt. Colonel "Angelina Mi Tilla"that she alone saved his life and got the medal of honor for her bravery. But this was to be tied down to problems in paperwork. When this commander was facing cancer alone. Msg. George Muddle of the Space Force became her friend. Commander Angelina Mi Tilla told George just one thing, "If I shall ever die please, George place my ashes on a rocket and scattered my ashes in space.

"George ---------------- I will do it"

This got the attention of a woman whom hired"George and Sheldon Muddle"To start working for her and her name is Bee Moon. This is the story on how they got on at Moon Space agency working on two rockets. Soon George Muddle would be throw right in going into outer space.

BACK ON THE SPACE STATION DEVON SIX III

Tension was building up between Dick M. McBride and Andrea McBride for being stuck. On the station waiting for a clear day to land and being home for the holidays. Thanksgiving in outer space was not good for this couple was fighting away from the kids. Then on one such time Dick M. McBride receives a called from Cape Canaveral. It was from Abner C. Peabody the head of NASA ground control who had a bold plan all ready to play out. So Dick M. started to listen and begin to think on it so much.

Then right after the call Dick started to look around and found some of the supplies were gone. So he asked Andrea about them and she told him it was for the kids.

That was the final straw for this one man and on another night in outer space he called NASA and talked to Abner alone and he would do it. "Leave his Wife and Kids in outer space four days before CHRISTMAS"To take the money offered to him and run and start a new life over again.

"NO MORE WIFE OR KID HAPPY DAYS FOR ME COMING TRUE "

CHAPTER V

BETRAYAL

"JUST BEING TRAPPED IN OUTER SPACE WITHOUT A WAY TO TALK OUT. It's the WORST HORROR FEELING OF ALL TIME AND I NEVER WANTED TO WISH THIS ON ANYONE "

Andrea Jones very own online journal

It happened on the night of December 21st. When Andrea and Dick had one very severe fight. That had very deep actions on them. It was all about the both of them had lost all true feelings of love. Toward each other and Dick went away to his own bed. To sleep and then Cape C. called it was from Abner C. Peabody asked about the plan that they alone was talked about in the past. Dick told him "Mr. Peabody All systems are a GO and let me do one thing up here.

Abner ---------"You wont regret it and the money will be waiting on your arrival Back on Earth"!

Then Dick Maynard McBride did the ultimate act of great horror to his wife and kid. He left them all alone in outer space and wrecked the com link.

So that no one can talked back to Cape Canaveral. This would go down to being a deep down low in being a super scum bag. Yet in Dick's own world he would get nearly five billion dollars in return. Then a new life away from Andrea and the kids. This will be a final act of divorce in marriage, yet this one man just made a deep mistake. Just didn't care anymore all he ever wanted was the deep money coming.

ON THE MORNING DEC. 21st. A NEW LIGHT BEGINS

Andrea Jones McBride woke up and found the commlink, wrecked and only life support monitors still on. There was no sight of Dick M. McBride and there was a handwritten note by him. That she read this note of deep and angry statement. That was taken in and it broke this very proud and beautiful woman. For she alone cried in silence and then wiped away all of her own tears. Now faced with a personal challenge,

Her inner strength of a heroine was so needed to come out. For she was awaken now and later she awoke the children and she lied about the fate of her husband and only father to their own child. Then lied to all and it was the only way to protect them and now the challenge was to find a way to call Cape Canaveral.

The older kids Andrew and Molly begin work on life support systems. While the two native children Little Bear and Beautiful Deer begin to work on finding supplies. The last child was her daughter and her name was Young Shiloh and she found something new that was brought it up. It was a modified flip phone and had only two numbers in place. At first Andrea never wanted to use it, because I was worried about survival that was means a lot.

That this one phone that was stowed away earlier for just in case of a emergency. Now it was happening now to the space station Devon Six.

Shiloh looked at the flip phone and one number was to Moon Space agency and the second, The White House in Washington DC. She tried to show this to Mom and it was no deal.

In the first day without that sorry guy named D. Andrea Jones begin making out her last will and testament and placed in a harden metal box. That was used for science and then there was the flip phone all ready for her to use. Then at her last minute she called the

White House number for fun and only to find out that. Her father was the President of the United States of America, This special time was a light in the darkest day of her life.

LIGHTS OF CHANGE II

The President answered first Andrea, Is that you there Andrea ======= Yes Dad I am here and I didn't know that you became President. I've haven't voted in anything for the last ten years. Then the President secretary butted in and told about a very important meeting coming up fast.

Just to found out now about the angry side of this President and got a very intense chewing out. Then the Secret Service agents were called into the oval office. There was four great men Amos and Moses were the tallest and biggest agents that were assigned to this man.

Sly and Arnold were the strongest agents and they all had only one order to follow. When the President talked out in the open. This one time gentleman would you please guard me while I answer and talked on the flip phone.

It is very important to me and I've just don't want anyone bugging me. All the agents agreed and for it was a rare deal to be called into the oval office. After the butt in by the sect. and the agents whom made sure not to ever interrupt the president ever again. He called on the flip phone and talked to someone very special and so close to the heart.

Andrea I am back and I made darn sure that no one will ever bothered me again. Please tell me what happen and we need to catch up on important things. Now Andrea talks to her father the first time in nearly nine years.

Hello Dad When I left you and I just got married to a man named Dick Maynard McBride. At first it was love at first sight, and then we had a one girl and her name is Shiloh. She was given this in honor of a great lady. That we both have so much respect for her. Then things begin to turn for the worst when Space travel came up and available. Dick became a space pilot and just loved it. Then he turned to a darker side and did things not right. But this sorry super scum bag of a man. Left his only daughter and me in outer space along with four other kids and there is two of them that belong to a man named both of them do call him. "GRANDPA""GREAT CHIEF "

They are his grandchildren and they are blind,just when The President seen with his own eyes the horror happening. He was so very MAD and he thrown a hard fist into a punching bag in the

Oval Office. Then he called in the Vice President into the room ASAP. Then he said to his daughter on the last message to her.

"YOU WILL BE COMING HOME ON CHRISTMAS DAY YOU WILL BE AT THE NORTH POLE"!

Vice President took over for the four days that the President was going to be away. This one mission to be happening was going to be a miracle for the time. That the world is needing a feel good story to be happening right here right now.

CHAPTER VI

GATHERING OF HEROES AND HEROINES

It was right after the first phone call that Andrea made to her father. Life was changing so very fast down on Earth. Her own father President Max Jones gathered all the very best secret service agents that was there and had a meeting with them. He called them all by name one by one and started talking to each agent.

Agent Chelsea Danger It was the first lady herself whom wanted you, Because just getting done with your secret service training and no where to go. Then you sit down by her at a park in the past. Wanting so much to protect the first lady and then got your wish. When she called the director and personally asked for you. The director had no choice and you came in to be. Ever since that time you have done so well."The Best of the Best"

Agent Sly ----------------"Yes Sir Mr. President "

Please Agent Sly I need to say this and I remember the first time, That I talked to you it was in a park and you was in a very bad mood.

Agent Sly ---------------- I remember that day Sir when I learned that, I didn't passed the Secret Service exam and I was so MAD, At the outside world and then I started talking to a man and he done a lot for me.

I do wish to thanked him for changing my own life here.

President ----------------- It was me on that day and I personally asked for you and the director again had no choice and you now came in. To this day you are one of the best Secret Service agents around.

Agent Sly ------------------ Thank You Mr. President.

Then the President started talking and he was going to wrapped it all up and let everyone know. How he felt about a hard deal that just came in.

Agents Amos and Moses I chosen you personally because of being brothers and Twins and to this day. Both of you have excel. "Never think that you are the last" "Just think that you are the very Best"

Agents Amos and Moses "Thank You Mr. President "

President ----------------------- Why I called you all in and why you are guarding the doors. I will tell you this, "I have learned that I have a grand daughter and she and her mother are in outer space aboard the space station "Devon Six "all alone and I am and the First Lady are going to get them down to earth on "Christmas Day at the North Pole "

All the agents say to the President --------------- Wow and Way cool and can we come along.

President ----------------------"Counting on it and I am going to need your help on this. Agent Danger,

Please get the first lady and tell her about this very"Top Secret"mission

FIRST CONTACT I

Special Agent Chelsea Danger went to the first lady and interrupted her meeting. When she heard of the news and she ran faster away than any agents at this time. For she admitted one thing from her past, I used to be a state champion before meeting the President and long before Andrea came in. "Most of the agents said Holy Cow "!

She is still fast ! The First lady called Moon Space agency and started to talking. To"Aunt Bee"personally since they were best friends in school a time back. The phone call came at a awkward time in Aunt Bee own life when her own nephew"Dr. Sage Moon"just gave his aunt a medical bill to this woman. In a rage Bee was and she told her nephew"

Get ready to go into outer space and cancel any more future medical appointments. Sage was so mad at his aunt for doing this to him. Then Bee reminded him about the medical school bill and the contract that was personally signed. But in a change of mood for the sake of own health. Bee told her nephew that by going into outer space that his contract will be paid in full. That he would be in the clear and was free to move anywhere in the world to setup his medical practice. Sage took this to be good news and he never made his"Aunt Bee MAD any more". In a great sign of respect to his Aunt, Sage reported to"GREAT CHIEF"to begin his space training along with George Muddle. Now the President finds the man known as "GREAT CHIEF ".

MEETING OF THE GREAT MEN II

It was upon the Native American Reservation that The President finding GREAT CHIEF during a vision quest. Right after the very private ceremony the men begin to talk. It was GREAT CHIEF that started first.

Your not the white father that disgraced me right after the explosion in outer space. When I came back down to earth a broken man being only one whom survived the disaster. That taken over four hundred lives. Now you are seeking me out and I've just don't want to trust you.

Now the President begins to speak and he has a flip phone that has a very important video on it. On this video GREAT CHEIF hears voices from his own past. Its the voices of GREAT CHIEF very own grandkids on a space station.

That makes him alone take a sudden notice to the man in front of him. That makes this one say something very bold.

"If this is a trick you are pulling on me, It is not very funny and you will not live another hour"!

President Jones is also so MAD and snaps back even harder.

"My own grand daughter is in outer space also, I am asking personally asked for your help to get them down. GREAT CHIEF

"I am sorry for the way I alone acted toward you"

"When can I go and get them down from outer space. You will not pay me no money. This will be my highest act of love I will be doing for my native nation.

"Sir if you do catch the ones who did this horrible act of evil, Can you send them to me right back at this reservation.

The President agreed to this very simple request from his equal. Then went a step further to insure that he was a man of his word. It was an executive order to be issued to promote more Native American events at the White House in the right month.

GREAT CHIEF personally took this as a sign of positive change and then said.

"We" will be heading to Cape Canaveral now.

Myself, George Muddle, Dr. Sage Moon and Night Bird.

President came back and said"You four will be in the back seat of a SR-74 planes and be at the Cape in under two hours time". There you will be meeting other members of the wild ones who are alrcady there.

"WHOA "

That is amazing The SR-74 is the last of the super fast jet plane. This one mission gentleman is of the highest priority. You will be getting them kids down to earth, The launch maybe rough at first, but in the end of it. You will be doing a miracle much needed at this time.

CHAPTER VII

THE WAR TO LEAVE

The time was December 22nd and everyone came to Cape Canaveral in Florida. Even all the members of the " Wild Ones were there in their rightful places. GREAT CHIEF, George Muddle, Dr. Sage Moon and his nurse " Elena " were there and ready to go in the rocket one. While " Night Bird, Slavonia a Russian nurse and pastor Artemis Miens was in rocket number two. They was all ready for launch and been in training for this day. That came without notice to everyone who was there.

MEANWHILE BACK CAPE CANAVERAL I

Aunt Bee was at the control booth ready to go and help out. She encountered Mission Director Abner C. Peabody who was trying his very best to stop this mission. But Aunt Bee alone had a backup plan and she put it in place. When the first lady was there and she begins to talking at Abner about a future launch. That is when Abner made his very evil plan and denied the launch. This bold act made the first lady so who was there alone very mad at him. That is Abner started to chew out the First Lady Brittany S.

Jones and Then the President showed up and called Abner to the office in the back. There was only two people there have seen the president in person in the past, Abner and GREAT CHIEF.

President Jones was not in a good mood at all after finding out about his only daughter and grand daughter was aboard that space station " Devon Six ". The man wanted answers and it was Secret Service agent Chelsea Danger just gave a smart phone that had very incredible proof of a hard and mean crime that was done. It seem to be a perfect, All it did was made this one man very madder than ever.

Then Agent Danger pulled out her service revolver and arrested Abner C. Peabody for attempted murder on the spot. At the front of the control panel at Cape Canaveral there was two space rockets getting ready to launch, They was waiting to get clearance in going. But it was the First Lady Brittany S. that alone gave the command to GO. She personally hit both launch buttons and they were going up right now, The rockets were named Angel's one and two are on there way to outer space.

LEAVING THE CAPE II

GREAT CHIEF and Night Bird just got done with the Check list and they was heading up at incredible speed. For both space rockets had a very secret cargo on the inside. That was going to be unveiled at the right time. Now there was a very fast race to reach the safe place very soon. In the rocket Angel One there is GREAT CHIEF, George Muddle and Dr. Sage Moon and his nurse. One member of the wild ones who would be the back up space pilot to take the rocket back to Cape Canaveral.

The rocket Angel two had on board Night Bird, Pastor Artemis and two members of the " Wild Ones " who was going to take over later and bring the space rockets back to home. For Pastor Artemis he had one amazing sermon to deliver on Christmas Day. For this one man had a very huge debt with " Aunt Bee " and by going up in Outer Space. His own debt with the billionaire would be free and in the clear.

Now both rockets have made into outer space and zero gravity took over. When it was clear to let one very soft thing out. Pastor Artemis let out a prayer in rocket two, While in rocket one George Muddle let his best friend go. It was the ashes of Lt. Commander Angelina Mi Tilla whom saved his own life in the past. Now this woman became an angel who would later helped both space crews.

In this one rescue mission of the highest priority. For these two men GREAT CHIEF AND Night Bird this space mission was about reconnecting with family. To deal with the evil one in their own family that place the native children in a bad place. While on the space station " Devon Six " Andrea gets a phone call on the flip phone that makes her day better. It was from her father the President, That there was two space rockets coming for her and she was to be coming home on Christmas day at the North Pole. Why the "North Pole Dad, on the landing " !

Her father answered with only this "I am going to fool the whole world and make them believe that Santa Claus does come from the North Pole" ! This is one time in my life that I 've just want a private family moment for all of us. Please honor my only request from you.

Those words said was the most beautiful of all time for this woman to hear. Then Andrea said to her father " Dad I love you "

The President said " Thank You that really means a lot to me here. " I have to go now and please get ready for a another phone call from the men " GREAT CHIEF and Night Bird "

They will be coming to you very soon and please get the kids ready to leave, I am looking forward to seeing you and Shiloh.

CHAPTER VIII

COMING HOME

The Space launch of Angels one and two was the roughest of all time. Yet this one time a greater spirit was with them. For when Astronaut George Muddle let his best friend ashes into space.

Commander Angelina Mi Tilla This was in the highest act of honor that anyone can do. That made his girl friend H. Mercy Miens fall more deeper in love with this man.

She said to " Aunt Bee " Moon " If he comes back I will be marrying that man " !

Aunt Bee ------------ " He will be back, He is with GREAT CHIEF and his son Night Bird "

They are the very best space pilots around and why they went up now I will tell you " Its very personal to both men " For GREAT CHIEF its his grandchildren and Night Bird its his nephew and niece. It was a ex brother in law that did the horrible thing by placing them kids in outer space. Now the ex is in tribal jail awaiting trial.

The news made H. Mercy Miens feel better about the great men soon to be heroes. Then she asked " Aunt Bee just one thing " When they come back may I give all men a hug " !

Aunt Bee -------------------- By all means YES DOCKING ON THE SPACE STATION " DEVON SIX "I

It was on the night of December 22nd when Andrea Jones just received a phone call on the flip phone. It was from Astronaut George Muddle letting her know that they are coming to bring everyone home. On Christmas day and they all will be landing at the North Pole. Why land at the North Pole !

Andrea Jones asked George Muddle this and he replied.

The President ordered us to touchdown at the North Pole. He said " You need a true CHRISTMAS "

One that you will not forget. Now we are coming up on your right and I have to go now and help GREAT CHIEF out in docking. Then Young Shiloh seen space shuttles come out from the rockets close by and it made Andrea say " Whoa, I don't believed this. These shuttles were smaller in size and yet had all the right things needed for a rescue. Then GREAT CHIEF and Night Bird did a space walk and fixed the air lock system and com links.

This was so needed before docking two shuttles together at the station. Now the two men went back to their shuttles and begin the process of docking. Space history was made when two shuttles docked at the same time. Devon Six the space station had two docking ports and at the time very ahead. Then it was GREAT

CHIEF made another call on the flip phone an hour later to Andrea letting her know about what is going to be happening very soon. That in order to keep it secret to the world the flip phone was the only thing to be used in talking.

DOCKED ON DECEMBER 22 The time 07:00.00 am GREAT CHIEF AND NIGHTBIRD had the smoothest docking ever and got the air locks opened on the space shuttles and was ready. To open the Space Station and meet Andrea and her daughter plus two other kids. Nightbird it was only niece and nephew that was first. The other kids was so happy that help was coming in.

Andrea got the phone call on the flip phone to open the air lock on the station. Then she meet GREAT CHIEF and NIGHTBIRD and she hugged both men and told of her story. Being abandoned on the station for a while and having to learned all about the space station. A whole new way of surviving the news made both men so very mad and yet she put the kids first. Before anything else and this made GREAT CHIEF say this to her.

" Andrea Jones you are always welcomed in all Native Nations and your daughter as well ". Doctor Sage begin to check out all the kids to see if they was fit to come home. They were so ready to leave and it was decided that Andrea and Shiloh be behind GREAT CHIEF and George Muddle, Dr. Sage and Elena. They would be in Angel One shuttle and the second would be Night Bird and the rest of the children. Pastor Artemis begin to pray because a Meteor shower was coming toward them. The prayer was for a safe passage away from that space station. He stayed inside the shuttle and this one ride he took would be the one that was not forgotten.

LEAVING DEVON SIX II

Noon time in Outer Space 12:00 Both shuttles were loaded and ready to leave when GREAT CHIEF and Night Bird said a a prayer to the GREAT SPIRIT. This was for a safe trip back down to Mother Earth. In a another orbit around Earth both craft seen a meteors take out the space station in a storm. That made the lead craft take defensive measures and Night Bird and his help from the group " Wild Ones as well " The shuttles had lasers on them and well charged and so ready. To fight for the right cause and it came clear that heading north was the safest way down. In Angel One shuttle George Muddle felt his best friend presence that really got to him. Then he alone remembered that Commander Angelina will fight tooth and nail for kids. Because she loved them so much.

For George Muddle the video game of the past " Asteroids is real to him " He was not going to lose this time. The stakes were just too high and he wanted so much to see his beloved H. Mercy Miens once more

CHAPTER IX

ENDING

Three days so have passed and it came upon the night of Christmas Eve. Both Space Shuttles have spend this time in outer space finding a way to get down to Earth. Then it came very clear that a North Pole landing was the only way. To bring both space craft down the safest way. While back down on earth, The President and First Lady both boarded a submarine in Alaska and it was on the way to the North Pole. It would get close to the pole and there was now radio and total silence on this trip.

Not even a cell phone was turned on, Then a plan of the Highest Secret was being worked out. While the Submarine so very close to the North Pole and there was silence. The Sub surface within a mile from the pole and it was very cold. There was a native tribe that had snowmobiles on hand and this helped out a lot.

NOW It was the President Jones came up with this plan. On Christmas day him and the First Lady would dress up as Mr. and Mrs. Santa Claus and they would both wave their hands to the world on this one day. Now for the shuttles coming in, There will be multiple Shuttles on a flyby to show the world a " Merry Christmas ". Then upon landing of the Shuttles all the extra sailors would come out and guard everyone there and give back privacy to me and plus the first lady

GREAT CHIEF and Night Bird they both have been thru so much.

Admiral Wayne asked the President just one thing.

" What is GREAT CHIEF 's full name !

The President said to all, GREAT CHIEF full name is

Chief " Wanaka Meanest Bear " USMC four time Medal of Honor winner and the only one living with this very highest honor. That is why all the Native Nations elected him to be the first leader. Then his son Night Bird a highly decorated navy seal team member also has a place in the native nation with great pride. Both men are reuniting with their own family and I asked you Admiral to give them privacy. The Admiral agreed to this order and made sure it happened.

Then there came a Sailor with a handwritten note, it said Both Shuttles are coming in the North Pole time in three hours from the south.

LANDING AT THE POLE I

At Cape Canaveral now " Aunt Bee Moon went on the Offensive to the world by letting all know. That her own shuttles were flying at near the North Pole. A Christmas flight to raise interest in future space launches also, This was done to cover up the main two Space Shuttles coming in from the south. These craft all had the holiday wishes posted on the sides in many languages. The outside world left them all alone and this one part of the President's plan was working. Then the first lady loved this looked of Mrs. Kris Kringle and this move was giving something very rare, " Privacy from the outside world ". Then the President done a Santa Suit and it really looked good on him. Which made him say to all " I 've love it when all of my plans come together "

COMING IN SIGHT II

It was Aunt Bee very own personal shuttle that she was on discovered Angels one and two. Headed right in sight. Then she had the pilots in the squad formed up in a angel pattern. Then GREAT CHIEF called her on the flip phone. He told her that everyone was fine and the gifts inside were also feeling great. Getting ready to land, I will be very busy for about two hours.

Aunt Bee ---------- OK

I 've just wanted to tell you in advance, You will be hugged by three women. A young little girl, A beautiful woman and the last a lady so close to Mother Earth.

GREAT CHIEF ------------ OK, I have to go now bye from here.

LANDING AT THE NORTH POLE III

Angels one and two made the smoothest landings ever and now they are near the North Pole. Safe and sound and Doctor Sage Moon went right away and checked everyone out. They were fine and Preacher Artemis had one very quick thing to say for all. Thank You "

The President and the First Lady now in a Santa suit and a long dress. They were in a snow machine heading toward both shuttles. Then another snow machine was getting setup for the sailors and Marines to come along in order. To give back one thing so true and needed " Privacy at this time ". Admiral Wayne made a phone call on the flip phone to GREAT CHIEF The sailors and Marines are there to make sure you get your privacy. This order comes from the President and I cannot changed it. They will not have cell phones or cameras on and no access to the internet.

GREAT CHIEF Wanaka ------------------- " Thank You "

NIGHT BIRD -------------------------------- " Thank You for me here as well "

SEEING SANTA at the North Pole IV

It was Andrea who came out of the Space Shuttle and looked around and couldn't believe. What her eyes just witness Santa Clause and Mrs. Clause just looked upon her and begin to cry. They haven't seen Andrea in over eight years and then came Shiloh who was with Doctor Sage. Both Santa and Mrs. Clause were in silence and because they have never seen Young Shiloh.

Suddenly A very fierce surge of pride came over them and both did surrendered to this beautiful moment. In time this would be the most beautiful CHRISTMAS gift they would ever received. Then Santa gave Andrea a handwritten note that would be her best gift ever.

The note read I am giving up politics to become a full time dad and a full time grandpa. Then Mrs. Clause Well she gave Andrea another gift from her own heart and she opened it. Just to find that it was a pair of long boots with a point at the front. This one gift made Andrea's feel better, But it was the handwritten note. Which became a treasured item and made her Christmas very special.

The other kids that was in the shuttle came out and played outside for a bit. Then they too was so very happy to be on the ground. After spending a time in outer space soon they was with the members of the " Wild Ones ".

Then it came to GREAT CHIEF and Night Bird who all alone spent time with the twin native children.

The twins let it be known that they never wanted to go back in outer space. This news made both men feel so much better. That there own fight into space was well worth it. Then GREAT CHIEF just got a new handwritten note. That the evil men who have done this very mean and horrible act were arrested and awaiting court on Native Land. Then Santa came by and asked to read the handwritten note and read it. Then he said to GREAT CHIEF " The Government will not interfere in this case, because of highest security reasons. If this got out in the open Space Travel would be shut down for good.

GREAT CHIEF and Santa agreed to this and Mrs. Clause spent time with Andrea and there was only one request to be made. That Shiloh time in outer space will not be recorded in history. Santa agreed to this request and Mrs. Clause was happy for her gift from the heart. That meant so much to her and then.

Andrea Jones came up to GREAT CHIEF and gave him a firm hug and said " Thank You for helping me get down from Space " This made the man feel good and the vision from Aunt Bee was coming true.

LEAVING THE NORTH POLE V

Both shuttles Angels one and two was refuel on the way of leaving. Everyone who was aboard them wanted to ride in the snow machines. It was the members of the " Wild Ones " that took the shuttles back into the sky and joined up with the other ten. The Submarine that was near the pole had left with Santa, Mrs. Clause, Andrea and Shiloh aboard.

They left the North Pole clean and no mess around, Then a snow storm came and wiped out any memories of the past.

GREAT CHIEF, Night Bird and the twins were in one snow machine leaving very fast. The second snow machine had every one else aboard. There were snow machines set up to trade places, Liked a memory of the pony express of a time ago.

NOW JUSTICE COMES

CHAPTER X

ENDING TO JUSTICE

The Submarine USS John Paul Jones had four very important guest aboard it now. The President and First Lady, Andrea Jones and young Shiloh Jones. There was still total silence and no cell phones or internet use. Because of the highest security risks involved. What took a toll on the crew sailors and marines was no cussing was also not allowed.

Now out of danger the Submarine made its way to safety and the four guest got off it. There was Aunt Bee Moon she was there along with Secret Service Agent Chelsea Danger. She was there to greet the President and report about the capture of three men behind this horrible deal. Then the First Lady made it clear to Agent Danger that she would be reassigned to be her protector after leaving the White House. Because she liked what Agent Chelsea has done for her and family. Plus Shiloh loved the idea of having a adopted big sister.

On the island GREAT CHIEF and Night Bird were there visiting with relatives. Then George Muddle was greeted by H. Mercy Miens and she kept her word on marriage. For she proposed to George and he said " YES" and then gave " GREAT CHIEF " a hard hug and the man turned red. For he felt the presence of " Mother Earth " upon him. Night Bird started to laugh and then was caught by surprise. When H. Mercy Miens gave him a hug as well and he fell down saying " WOW "

She asked GREAT CHIEF to marry her and George and he agreed to it. Then back at the Cape Canaveral.

A video call came to Aunt Bee from her staff that was very secured and Sheldon Muddle was so very proud of his big brother being a hero. Then Howard became Sheldon's best friend and those two made a connection of highest respect. Howard got married and his wife loved comic books and sci-fi as well.

Then a phone call came in and it was GREAT CHIEF it was from the courtroom. That the three men in this horrible deal were convicted found guilty.

Sentence to six life sentences each and to be placed at Lonely Rock Prison on Native land. This prison was maximum security and no chance of ever leaving. There was no parole ever to be granted to them ever.

IN THE END I

Andrea Jones gave up her smart phone for two reasons. To reconnect with her father and mother and spend a lot more time with them. The second reason was for young Shiloh to be spend a lot of time with her. President Jones did give up politics and endorsed a Latino American born candidate for President " Hector Poncho Martinez "

Our story continues in " The Darkest Hour "